Country Chipmunk
and
City Chipmunk

 Book Six

DISNEP PRESS
New York

Printed in China

First Edition
1 3 5 7 9 10 8 6 4 2

ISBN 978-1-4231-4901-9
T425-2382-5-11127

For more Disney Press fun,
visit www.disneybooks.com

ONCE UPON A TIME, there was a chipmunk who lived in a busy city. One day he decided to visit his friend in the country. So he packed up a few things and set off.

"Ahhh," he said as he went on his way. "What clean, fresh air! What beautiful trees! It must be nice to live in the country."

Before long, the city chipmunk arrived at the country chipmunk's house.

"Come in, come in!" exclaimed the country chipmunk. "You must be hungry. I will fix you a proper country meal."

As it happened, the city chipmunk *was* a bit hungry—and tired—after his trip. So he was quite happy to take a seat in a cozy chair by the fire while his friend made him something to eat.

At last dinner was ready. The country chipmunk brought one steaming plate after another into the dining room.

"These are my specialties," he said proudly, uncovering each plate. "Toasted chestnuts, toasted acorns, and toasted seeds!"

The city chipmunk smiled and tried to look excited. But in truth, he was disappointed. He had much fancier foods to choose from at home. Didn't the country chipmunk have anything more exciting to eat than nuts and seeds, he wondered.

The city chipmunk politely ate all of the food
he had been served. At the end of the meal, he
turned to his host.

"Don't you ever get tired of eating such plain
and simple foods all the time?" he asked.

The country chipmunk gave him a puzzled look. "What do you mean?" he asked. "What else is there?"

"What else is there?" replied the city chipmunk in disbelief.

The city chipmunk jumped up and ran to the other side of the table.

"You won't believe all there is to eat in the city," he told his friend.

Just then the city chipmunk had an idea. He invited the country chipmunk to visit his home and learn about city life.

The country chipmunk hesitated for a moment. After all, his friend had just arrived. There were so many things to do in the country. They hadn't even gone hay-jumping yet! But the city chipmunk looked very eager, so the country chipmunk agreed.

The next morning, right after a breakfast of acorn cereal, the city chipmunk and the country chipmunk set off together on the long journey to the city.

By lunchtime, they had reached the city chipmunk's home. It was in a tall tree behind a large house.

Someone honked a car horn below. *Beep! Beep!* Then a helicopter flew by overhead.

"Wow!" cried the country chipmunk. "So much hustle and bustle! How exciting it must be to live in a city."

The country chipmunk was even more impressed when he followed the city chipmunk into his neighbor's house and saw the amazing pantry. It was filled with cheeses, jams, honey, peanut butter, cookies, candies, cakes, and a

variety of other treats. The country chipmunk had never seen so many different foods! He couldn't wait to try them all!

The chipmunks climbed up into the pantry. The city chipmunk offered his friend a taste of peanut butter. It stuck to the roof of his mouth, and it was several minutes before he could speak again.

Then his friend led him to three different fruit jams.

"Which do you like best?" asked the city chipmunk. "Blueberry? Strawberry? Peach?"

"Mmm!" said the country chipmunk. "They are all delicious. How could you ever choose just one favorite?"

The country chipmunk patted his stomach. He was starting to feel full. But the city chipmunk was just getting started.

Next the city chipmunk scampered over to a big container of honey. The country chipmunk followed, and together they managed to pull the honey off the shelf.

The city chipmunk squeezed the bottle and honey flew everywhere! But the chipmunks didn't care. They filled their tummies even more with its supersweet, golden, ooey-gooey goodness.

"Yum!" cried the country chipmunk. "This is even better than the jam. You must be the luckiest chipmunk ever!"

The city chipmunk agreed. But he *still* wasn't done!

The city chipmunk jumped down to the next shelf and pulled out two cookies.

"This one is chocolate chip, and this one is oatmeal raisin. What do you think?" he asked his friend.

"Fantastic!" the country chipmunk exclaimed. "I've never tasted anything so wonderful. I could get used to eating like this!"

As the words left the country chipmunk's mouth, the owner of the house opened the pantry to get a soda. He spotted the two chipmunks at once.

"That rotten chipmunk again! And this time he has a friend. Get out of my pantry," the owner shouted. "How many times do I have to tell you?"

The owner of the house picked up a broom and begin swatting at the chipmunks.

The city chipmunk and the country chipmunk scurried through the open window and across the backyard. They scampered up the tree and into the city chipmunk's home.

They had not been inside more than a minute when the country chipmunk gathered his things and said, "Well, thanks so much for everything, but I must be getting home now."

"What?" replied the city chipmunk. "You just got here. And what about all the delicious food? Didn't you like it?"

"Oh, yes, I did," said the country chipmunk. "But I'd rather eat my simple food in peace than have to face that angry fellow in order to get my meals!"

So the country chipmunk said good-bye to
his friend and began to walk back to the country.
The city chipmunk stayed in the city with his
fancy foods. The chipmunks had enjoyed their
adventures, but they realized they were happiest
in their own homes.